SWEET VALLEY KIDS

# BOSSY STEVEN

Written by
Molly Mia Stewart

Created by
FRANCINE PASCAL

Illustrated by
Ying-Hwa Hu

D0062931

A BANTAM SKYLARK BOOK
NEW YORK · TORONTO · LONDON · SYDNEY · AUCKLAND

RL 2, 005–008

BOSSY STEVEN
*A Bantam Skylark Book / May 1991*

*Sweet Valley High® and Sweet Valley Kids are registered trademarks of Francine Pascal*

*Conceived by Francine Pascal*

*Produced by Daniel Weiss Associates, Inc.*
*33 West 17th Street*
*New York, NY 10011*

*Cover art by Susan Tang*

*Skylark Books is a registered trademark of Bantam Books, a division of Bantam Doubleday Dell Publishing Group, Inc. Registered in U.S. Patent and Trademark Office and elsewhere.*

ISBN 0-553-15881-3

*Published simultaneously in the United States and Canada*

Bantam Books are published by Bantam Books, a division of Bantam Double-day Dell Publishing Group, Inc. Its trademark, consisting of the words "Bantam Books" and the portrayal of a rooster, is Registered in U.S. Patent and Trademark Office and in other countries. Marca Registrada. Bantam Books, 666 Fifth Avenue, New York, New York 10103.

PRINTED IN THE UNITED STATES OF AMERICA

OPM      0 9 8 7 6 5 4 3 2 1

# A Deal Is a Deal

"You're not really going to make us clean your room, Steven, are you?" Jessica asked. "Mom? Can he make us do that?"

"A deal is a deal," Mrs. Wakefield answered.

"Yes, but . . ." Jessica said.

"A week isn't that long," Elizabeth said. "It won't be so bad. Steven doesn't have *that* many chores."

"I have a lot more than you know about," Steven said, grinning.

Jessica and Elizabeth looked at each other. Losing the bet was beginning to sound worse by the second!

*To Jenna Weinstein*

# CHAPTER 1

# First Prize

It was science day at Sweet Valley Elementary School. Elizabeth Wakefield looked around the school gym. She saw tables covered with projects created by students in the upper grades. Almost everyone in school was there, and the gym was very noisy.

"Isn't this fun?" Elizabeth asked her twin sister, Jessica.

"I guess so," Jessica said. But it sounded like she didn't mean it.

Elizabeth knew that science wasn't her sister's favorite subject. It wasn't hers, either. Of all the subjects in their second-grade class, Elizabeth liked reading best. But she was happy to be there. And she was excited that their older brother, Steven, had a project on display. Steven was in the fourth grade and this was his first science fair.

Elizabeth and Jessica were identical twins. They looked the same on the outside but they were very different inside. Elizabeth loved school. Jessica preferred recess and sharing secrets with her friends. After school, Elizabeth liked to play adventure games outside or practice soccer. Jessica liked to play with her dolls and stuffed animals indoors.

Both girls had blue-green eyes and long blond hair with bangs. The only way to tell them apart was to look at the name bracelets they wore. Jessica liked to wear pink clothing, and Elizabeth liked to wear green.

Even though they were very different, Elizabeth and Jessica loved being twins. They shared a bedroom, they shared candy, and each twin often knew just what the other was thinking. They were best friends.

"Come on, let's go see if Steven won," Jessica said as they passed a project called "Planets in the Ocean."

"I hope he wins, but I don't want him to win our bet," Elizabeth said.

"Me, too," Jessica said.

Steven had bragged to the twins that he would win first place with his volcano project. Jessica had made a bet with him. If Steven won, the twins would do his chores around the house for a week. If the twins won, he would have to do their chores.

"Hi, girls!" Mrs. Wakefield said when Elizabeth and Jessica arrived at Steven's table. Mr. Wakefield was helping Steven tape down his sign that explained how the volcano worked.

"They're going to judge my project now," Steven said. "I know mine's the best."

Jessica stuck her tongue out at Steven. Elizabeth didn't say anything. She knew he was bragging because he was nervous.

Finally the judges arrived at Steven's table.

"Does this erupt?" a woman asked. She looked closely at the volcano. It was made out of papier-mâché.

Steven spoke in his most grown-up voice as he showed her how his model volcano worked. First he poured baking soda down the opening. Then he added vinegar, and the

volcano appeared to erupt. Elizabeth listened to the speech he had been practicing for many days, and she felt proud of him. She thought he deserved to win, even if it meant extra work for her and Jessica.

"Cross all your fingers so that we win," Jessica whispered in Elizabeth's ear.

"But if we win, Steven loses," Elizabeth whispered back.

Jessica grinned. "I know."

"But his experiment is so good," Elizabeth said.

"It is," Jessica agreed. "But I don't want to do his work. He can win second or third place."

Elizabeth watched while three of the science teachers stepped up to the microphone. "Ladies and gentlemen, boys and girls," said

6

Mrs. Patterson, a sixth-grade teacher. "Can I have your attention please?"

Everyone stopped talking. Elizabeth looked at Steven and smiled.

"I'd like to start with the fourth-grade entries," Mrs. Patterson said. "It was difficult to decide between all the outstanding experiments. But after discussing it very carefully with my co-judges, we've decided to award the first place ribbon to . . ."

Elizabeth held her breath and squeezed her eyes shut. She didn't care how many chores she had to do. She wanted her brother to win.

"Steven Wakefield and his Miracle Volcano!"

# CHAPTER 2

# A Deal Is a Deal

"Hooray!" the whole Wakefield family shouted at the same time. Mrs. Wakefield hugged Steven and then she hugged Elizabeth and Jessica.

"I won!" Steven said. "I won, I won, I won!"

"Congratulations," Mr. Wakefield said. He shook Steven's hand. "We're very proud of you."

Jessica was excited for her brother now, but she was disappointed, too. She and Elizabeth had lost the bet.

"OK, you two," Steven said. "You have to do whatever I say for one whole week."

"That's fine with me," Elizabeth said cheerfully. "You won our bet fair and square."

Jessica wasn't as happy. "Oh, brother," she said with a sigh. "I wish we had never made this bet at all."

"You deserve a special dinner," Mrs. Wakefield said to Steven.

After all the prizes had been awarded, the family walked out to the parking lot. Steven held his blue ribbon high in the air. He began to think about his celebration dinner. "I want cheeseburgers, fries, apple pie with ice cream, pizza—"

"Whoa!" Mr. Wakefield said with a laugh. "We're having one dinner, not ten!"

"And I don't want to be cooking all night,"

9

Mrs. Wakefield said. She put her arm around Steven's shoulder. "I was just thinking of the mousetrap you built. Remember how it caught our runaway hamster?"

"Yes," Steven said. "Jessica and Elizabeth would have gotten into a lot of trouble without me." His shoebox mousetrap had caught the twins' class hamster. The pet had escaped from its cage at the Wakefields' home.

Steven caught up to Jessica and Elizabeth. "You know, I had to work so hard on my experiment that I couldn't clean my room all week."

Jessica gasped. "We can't clean a whole week's worth of mess," she said. "Mom? Is that fair?"

"A deal is a deal," Mrs. Wakefield said.

Jessica looked at her father with a pleading expression. "Dad? Can he do that?"

Mr. Wakefield was a lawyer, so he knew all about making deals. "Hmm . . ." he said, as he opened the car doors. "I don't want to take this to court, but my opinion is . . ."

Jessica and Elizabeth looked worried while their father thought things over. The bet was beginning to sound worse and worse by the second!

"Since you didn't decide in advance that you would do new chores only, my opinion is, you're stuck with Steven's old chores," Mr. Wakefield said. "I'm sorry."

"Two victories in one day!" Steven said. "It sure will be nice to sleep in a super-clean room tonight."

"For the first time in a long time," Mr. Wakefield teased.

"I hope you girls will be able to get into the room," Mrs. Wakefield added. "I can't find a

11

clear space on the floor for the vacuum cleaner."

"I guess it was a dumb idea to make the bet," Elizabeth said to Jessica.

"Really dumb," Jessica agreed.

Steven climbed into the car. "Don't slam the door when you get in. It hurts my ears."

"Steven!" Mrs. Wakefield scolded.

Jessica got into the car and gave her brother a big smile. Then she slammed the car door as hard as she could.

# CHAPTER 3

# Work, Work, Work

"Whose turn is it to set the table?" Mrs. Wakefield asked as she began to make Steven's special dinner.

Steven smiled. "Mine," he said. He looked at the twins. "So I guess that makes it your turn."

"I'll do it," Elizabeth said. She opened the silverware drawer and began to take out forks and knives and spoons.

"Don't forget to fold the napkins nicely," Steven added.

Mrs. Wakefield looked at Elizabeth and

said gently. "Remember, it's only for a week and that's not very long at all."

"I don't mind," Elizabeth said. "It's not that bad."

"A week is seven long, long days," Jessica said. "But at least he can't make us do his homework."

When dinner was ready, they all sat down at the dining room table.

"Look at those fries," Mr. Wakefield said, rubbing his hands together. "They look great. Pass the ketchup, please."

Elizabeth looked around the table. The ketchup wasn't there. She saw Steven looking at her. He silently pointed his thumb toward the kitchen.

"I'll get it," Elizabeth said.

As soon as she brought the ketchup back

and sat down, Mrs. Wakefield noticed that the salt and pepper were missing.

"I'll go," Elizabeth said, popping out of her chair again.

"No, don't get up," her mother said. "Steven, would you get the salt and pepper, please?"

Steven picked up a french fry and waved it in the air. "Jessica can do it for me."

"What?" Jessica stopped her fork halfway to her mouth and stared at him. "Why me?"

"A deal's a deal," Steven said.

Mr. Wakefield looked at Jessica. "Your brother is one tough customer," he said.

Jessica made a face at Steven, and then got up and stomped out to the kitchen. When she came back, Elizabeth gave her a sympathetic smile. They both watched Steven help himself to a second hamburger.

"Don't forget about cleaning my room later," Steven said between bites. "After one of you takes my turn helping Dad with the dishes."

"But I was going to watch TV," Jessica wailed. "My favorite movie is on, and it starts right after dinner! Liz, could you help Dad?"

Elizabeth looked at her sister and frowned. Jessica tried to get out of doing chores as much as Steven did. Most of the time, Elizabeth helped Jessica out. But if she had to do her own chores, plus Steven's, plus Jessica's share, she wouldn't have time to do anything else.

"Jessica, you can help with the dishes," Mr. Wakefield said firmly. "We'll give them a quick rinse and stick them in the dishwasher while Liz gets a start on Steven's room. If you two work together, you will be finished in time for the movie."

"If they do a good enough job," Steven said smiling.

Jessica slumped down in her chair.

"We will," Elizabeth told him.

"I'm sure you will, too," Mrs. Wakefield said. "And I'll be the one to decide, not Steven. I don't want him working you two into exhaustion."

Steven took a sip of his milk and laughed. "This is the best bet I ever won," he said.

Elizabeth and Jessica looked at each other. They both knew it was going to be the worst week of their lives.

# CHAPTER 4

# The Meanest Brother in the World

"I'm never speaking to him again in my whole life," Jessica said on Saturday morning. She hung upside down from the jungle-gym bars and crossed her arms.

"He sure is being a pain," Elizabeth said from the next bar.

Below them, Lila Fowler and Eva Simpson were hanging by their hands. Ellen Riteman and Amy Sutton were looking up from below.

"You know what he made us do last night?" Jessica went on. "He made us make his bed twice because it wasn't neat enough the first time. Then we had to clean his whole room."

"Yuck," Lila said. "I would never clean someone else's room."

"You never even have to clean your own room," Jessica reminded her friend. She knew that Lila's parents were wealthy and had a live-in housekeeper.

Elizabeth shook her head. "But we had to. We made a bet."

"I know what you could do," Eva said.

"What?" Jessica asked eagerly. Eva always had good ideas.

"You could make another bet with Steven. One you know you could win," Eva suggested.

Jessica frowned as she thought about that. It was a good idea, but she couldn't think of

any other kind of bet she and Elizabeth could make. And what if they made another bet and *lost*? Then they might have to do chores for two weeks instead of one.

"You could bet you could name more colors than he could," Ellen said. "Or more animals."

"That's no good," Elizabeth said. "Steven knows a lot of animals."

"You could have a spelling contest," Amy said.

Jessica looked at Amy and shook her head. "No way. Then I'd really lose. I have to think of—wait! I know!"

The others looked at Jessica.

"What?" Elizabeth asked.

"Dad's birthday is next week," Jessica said. "We could see who makes him the better birthday present."

Elizabeth frowned. "Dad would never say that one present was better than the other."

"That's right," Eva said. "My father always likes all his presents equally."

Jessica sat up on the bar then dropped onto the ground. "Well I'm going to think of something," she said grumpily. "I don't want Steven bossing me around all week."

"Shhh!" Lila said. "Here he comes!"

Jessica watched as her brother walked over. She could already tell he was going to act bossy and know-it-all in front of her friends.

"I just remembered something," Steven said when he was in front of Elizabeth and Jessica. "I told Dad I would help him clean out the garage today."

"So?" Jessica asked.

"So, you're doing my chores for a week, and I want you to do it for me," he said.

"No!" Jessica shouted. "I'm playing with my friends."

Steven shook his head slowly. "You made a bet and you have to do it."

Jessica was angry. It was too nice a day to go home and clean the garage. More than anything, she wanted to stay and play with the others.

"I'll help Dad," Elizabeth said. She climbed down from the bars and wiped her hands on her pants.

"Do I have to go with you?" Jessica asked.

Elizabeth looked at the ground and shrugged. "No. I'll do it by myself if you want to stay."

"Thanks!" Jessica said. She felt bad about not helping Elizabeth. Elizabeth had also

24

done most of the work cleaning Steven's room. "I'll do the next job," she said.

"Promise?" Elizabeth asked.

Instead of answering, Jessica crossed her heart and snapped her fingers twice. That was their secret promise signal.

Jessica still didn't want to do any of Steven's chores, though. She decided that she was going to figure out a way to get out of doing them at all.

# CHAPTER 5

# Elizabeth's Plan

Elizabeth jumped off her bike and went around to the backyard. Her father was sitting by the swimming pool. "Hi, Dad!" she called out.

"Hi, honey. Back so soon?" Mr. Wakefield asked.

"I'm helping you clean out the garage," Elizabeth said.

Her father looked surprised. "I thought Steven—Oh, I see," he said with a smile. "You're certainly being a good sport about this. Where's Jessica?"

"She wanted to stay at the park," Elizabeth said. "I can do her share, though. Then she'll help me next time."

"That's very nice of you," her father said. "Ready to get some work done?"

The garage door made a rumbling sound as it rolled up. Elizabeth began by organizing cans of paint by color, while Mr. Wakefield filled a garbage bag with junk.

"We don't need this anymore, do we?" Mr. Wakefield asked. He was holding up a broken baby walker.

"No." Elizabeth giggled. "What about this?" She held up a dusty paintbrush with no bristles on it.

Mr. Wakefield scratched his head and pretended to think. "Hmmmm. I don't know."

"Maybe we should ask Mom," Elizabeth teased. She threw out the paintbrush. Next, she looked for a broom. The garage floor was dirty, and the more Elizabeth swept, the more dusty it seemed to get.

"This sure is hot and dusty work," her father said. He wiped his forehead with his shirt sleeve. "You know where I would like to be? On a fishing trip. Then every time we felt hot we could dive into a nice cool lake. That's what Grandpa Wakefield and I used to do."

Elizabeth stopped sweeping and listened. It was always fun to hear stories about her father as a little boy.

"Did you go fishing a lot?" she asked.

"Yes. And Grandma would make her homemade lemonade," Mr. Wakefield went on happily. "It was as good as the lemonade you and Jess made." Elizabeth smiled as she remembered the lemonade stand she and Jessica had set up. "Then she would whip up

28

a batch of cookies," Mr. Wakefield added. "I'd be in heaven."

"Cookie heaven," Elizabeth said with a giggle.

Suddenly, Elizabeth had a great idea. She knew what she and Jessica could do for their father's birthday. It would be better than anything Steven could think of! She couldn't wait for Jessica to come home so she could tell her.

"I think we should stop and have something to drink," Mr. Wakefield said. "All this talk about lemonade and cookies is making me thirsty."

"And hungry," Elizabeth added.

As they walked out into the driveway, Jessica rode up on her bike. "Hi," she called out.

"Perfect timing, Jessica," their father

joked. "We were just going inside for refreshments."

Elizabeth tapped her sister on the shoulder as they started walking to the house. "Wait a second," she whispered.

They let Mr. Wakefield get ahead of them. Jessica looked puzzled. "What is it?" she asked.

"I have an idea," Elizabeth said. "You know how Dad always talks about the great homemade things Grandma Wakefield used to bake all the time?"

Jessica nodded quickly. "Sure. I love it when she brings some on visits."

"Well, what if we bake a birthday cake for Dad. He'd really really love it," Elizabeth said.

"That's a perfect plan!" Jessica looked excited. "And Steven would never think of

31

doing that. Our present will be much better than his."

"Then he'll have to stop showing off," Elizabeth said.

"And bossing us around," Jessica added.

The two girls looked at each other and smiled. "Come on, let's go inside," Elizabeth said.

Suddenly, both girls froze in their tracks. Steven was coming out of the garage.

"Did you hear what we were talking about?" Elizabeth asked.

"Were you spying on us?" Jessica demanded.

Steven shrugged. "I was putting my bike away. Why would I want to spy on you?" he said. "Besides, I have more important things to do."

"Come on," Elizabeth said quietly to

Jessica. They turned and headed for the house. Elizabeth looked over her shoulder at their brother.

Had he heard their plan?

# CHAPTER 6

# The Baking Contest

Jessica peeked into the kitchen after dinner on Sunday.

"The coast is clear," she whispered, waving to Elizabeth. They tiptoed in and went to the counter shelf where their mother kept the cookbooks.

"Here's *Forty Fabulous Cakes*," Elizabeth said as she pulled out a heavy book.

Jessica looked over Elizabeth's shoulder to make sure no one was coming. "Look up double-chocolate seven-layer cherry cake," she said.

"That sounds too hard," Elizabeth said.

She opened the book to a page in the middle. "How about a coconut pound cake?"

Jessica made a face. "Daddy doesn't like coconut, remember?" She got closer to Elizabeth and flipped through the pages fast. "His favorite kind is—"

"Shh! I hear someone!" Elizabeth whispered.

"Oops!" Jessica closed the book quickly and hid it behind her back just as Steven walked into the kitchen.

"What are you doing?" he asked.

Jessica smiled innocently. "Nothing," she said.

"One of you has to take the newspapers out tonight. The recycling truck comes tomorrow," Steven said. He tried to look behind Jessica, but she was able to keep the book out of sight.

Jessica waited until he left the room and then she looked at Elizabeth. "Our plan is working," she said.

Mr. Wakefield always left for work early on Monday mornings. "I hope you all remember what's happening on Wednesday," Mrs. Wakefield said at breakfast.

"We do," Jessica said quickly. She was hoping that Steven didn't know what Mrs. Wakefield was talking about.

Steven took a big gulp of his orange juice. "Do you mean Dad's birthday?" he asked in his know-it-all voice. "I'd never forget. I'm making him the best birthday present. I'm going to make him a birthday cake."

"WHAT?" Elizabeth shouted.

"You stole our idea!" Jessica said angrily. "You *were* spying on us!"

37

Steven took a bite of his toast and didn't say a word.

"Mom!" Jessica said, turning to their mother. "That was our idea. It's not fair."

Mrs. Wakefield looked thoughtful. "Well, why don't you bake two different cakes. I'll be here to help you."

"We don't want any help," Elizabeth spoke up. "We want to do it by ourselves."

"I don't need any help either," Steven said with a big smile. "Elizabeth and Jessica are going to do all the hard work for me."

"The bet was only for chores," Jessica pointed out. "Dad's birthday isn't a chore."

Steven didn't answer. He just stood up and walked out of the kitchen.

"Mom? That's not fair, is it?" Elizabeth asked in a worried voice.

Mrs. Wakefield shook her head. "No, it

certainly is not. I'll have a talk with Steven. If he wants his cake to be from *him*, he has to do all the work himself."

Jessica felt better. She knew their cake would be better than Steven's. *Soon,* she thought, *Steven won't be bossy Steven anymore.*

# CHAPTER 7

# Angel Food Cake

"We have to choose our recipe," Elizabeth said, when she and Jessica got to the bus stop.

Jessica practiced a modern dance pose. "How about an upside-down cake?" she asked. She leaned over and looked at Elizabeth from between her legs.

"Upside-down Jessica," Elizabeth giggled. She took out the cookbook from her schoolbag and looked at the pictures again. There were gooey chocolate cakes and fruit cakes, vanilla almond cakes and peppermint-stick cakes. There were cakes she had never seen before.

"What are you looking at?" asked a voice behind her.

Elizabeth looked up. It was Todd Wilkins, one of her classmates. "We're making Dad's birthday cake," she explained. "We have until Wednesday."

"I'm a good cook. My favorite is marble cake with confetti frosting," Todd said.

"Look at this one," Jessica said. She pointed to a picture of a fancy wedding cake with flowers made out of pink and white frosting.

"I think Dad's favorite is angel food cake," Elizabeth said. "That's what we should make."

"We're his little angels," Jessica said in a singsong voice.

"Have you ever made a cake before?" Todd asked.

Elizabeth and Jessica shook their heads no.

"I have," Todd went on. "It tasted great but I messed up the frosting. I got little bits of cake crumbs in it."

"Are you picking out the cake I should make?" Steven asked as he strolled up.

Elizabeth slammed the book shut. "Mom says you have to make your cake yourself."

"Big deal. It's easy," Steven said, shrugging his shoulders. "All you have to do is throw a bunch of ingredients in a bowl, stir them and cook the batter. I'm making a special chocolate cake. It'll be even better than the one in the magazine because I'm going to add secret ingredients."

Elizabeth and Jessica and Todd all looked

at one another. They all thought Steven was being a show-off.

"Sure, it's easy," Jessica repeated. "We'll just see how easy it is when you do it."

"It's easy for an expert like me," Steven said. "And don't forget. You still have to do all my chores until the end of the week."

"Oh, yeah?" Jessica said. "Well, I have an idea." She stood in front of Steven and pointed one finger at him. "If our cake is better than yours, you have to do our chores."

"Forget it," Steven said. "I'm not betting that."

Elizabeth stood next to her sister. "How about if our cake is better, the first bet is off and we don't have to do any more chores?"

"That sounds fair," Todd spoke up. He looked at Steven. "Why don't you take the bet?"

"You're not afraid you'll lose, are you?" Jessica asked.

"Don't forget, Steven," Elizabeth teased, "there's no way you could ever lose a bet with us. You're an expert at everything."

Steven made a face. "Ha ha ha. OK. The first bet is off if your cake is better than mine," he said. "But if it's a tie then you still lose."

"Deal," Elizabeth said.

Steven started to walk away, but he stopped to look back at them. "Oh, don't forget. After school one of you has to get the leaves and stuff out of the swimming pool. See you later, shrimps."

He walked away to talk to his friends.

"I bet you'll make a better cake," Todd said to Elizabeth.

Elizabeth smiled at Todd. "I bet we will, too."

"We'd better," Jessica said. "Or Steven will never, ever stop teasing us about it."

# CHAPTER 8

# The Big Bake-Off

Jessica and Elizabeth raced home from the bus stop on Wednesday. Steven walked slowly behind them.

"Hurry up," Steven teased. "You'll need lots of time to make the perfect cake."

"Don't pay any attention to him," Elizabeth said as they opened the front door. "I know we can do it."

When they ran into the kitchen, Mrs. Wakefield gave them a quick hug. "Ready, chefs?" she asked.

"Ready!" Jessica shouted. She grabbed the

cookbook and opened it to the angel food cake recipe.

Steven walked into the kitchen. "Here I am," he said. "Step aside so the expert can have some room."

"Steven," their mother said. "Cooking is serious business. I hope you won't clown around this afternoon. I took out the ingredients and utensils all of you will need. I also turned the oven on to preheat it. Do any of you have questions?"

Steven, Jessica, and Elizabeth shook their heads no.

"You're all set, then," Mrs. Wakefield said. "If you do need help, I'll be in the den."

"Thanks," Elizabeth and Jessica said at the same time.

Jessica decided to ignore her brother. She walked past him to put the cookbook on the countertop. She started to read the list of ingredients needed for their cake.

"Ten eggs," she said.

Elizabeth took one of the cartons of eggs their mother had put on the countertop. "Check."

"All-purpose flour," Jessica read off.

"Check," Elizabeth said.

Steven laughed. "Kids," he said, rolling his eyes. He pushed up his sleeves. "Anyone can follow a recipe. The trick is to add your own stuff."

"Sugar," Jessica said as she turned her back on him.

Elizabeth nodded. "Check."

"Let's start," Jessica said eagerly. She read the recipe. "It says we just use the egg whites. I know how to separate the eggs. Mom showed me once."

49

"I'll get a bowl." Elizabeth was about to take the large bowl that was stacked on top, but Steven also reached for it. "Excuse me," Elizabeth said.

Steven ignored her and grabbed the mixing bowl. Elizabeth took another one. Jessica opened the carton of eggs and took one out. "Here I go," she said.

She tapped the egg on the side of the bowl so that the shell cracked. The egg white came out of the shell, while the yolk stayed inside.

"I did it!" she said, picking up another egg. She cracked it again. This time the whole egg dropped into the bowl. "Oops."

Steven laughed. "Babies."

"I'll help," Elizabeth said. The twins started separating the eggs, but no matter how careful they were, some of the yolks and some of the shell fell in. Elizabeth carefully picked out the shells, and Jessica scooped the yolks out with a spoon.

"I think it's OK," Elizabeth said. She glanced over at Steven. He was mixing sugar, flour, and eggs together with a large wooden spoon.

"We have to beat the whites," Jessica read from the book. "That's easy."

While Elizabeth got the eggbeater, Jessica sneaked a look at her brother. He saw her and turned his back to hide his cake batter. "Don't look," he said.

"I'm ready," Elizabeth said. She turned the handle of the eggbeater. The egg whites began to swirl together and turn foamy.

"That looks easy," Jessica said with a big smile. "Let me try."

Jessica took the beater and turned the

handle even faster than Elizabeth. The egg whites rose higher. Just then the bowl slipped. The two extra eggs rolled off the counter and onto the floor. Jessica lifted the beater and the mixture began to splatter everywhere.

"Hey!" Steven yelled, wiping the back of his neck.

Jessica put the beater down inside the bowl. Elizabeth measured the sugar and vanilla and put them into the bowl. "Hurry up," Jessica whispered. "I want to finish before Steven does."

"I'll get the flour," Elizabeth said. She reached for it just as Steven reached for a bottle of chocolate syrup. The syrup tipped over, and Elizabeth dropped the bag of flour.

"Watch out!" Steven said.

"*You* watch out!" Elizabeth said.

Before she realized it, Jessica raised the beater too high again and another spray of egg whites went onto the counter. "Oh, no!" she wailed.

When she stepped back, she bumped into Steven. He spilled a cupful of sugar on the floor. "Look what you made me do!" he shouted.

"Me?" Jessica asked. "You got in my way!"

Even with the mess they were making, Jessica and Elizabeth followed their recipe very carefully. They could see that Steven was just making things up as he went along.

"What are your secret ingredients?" Elizabeth asked Steven.

"I can't tell you," Steven answered. He was pouring two cups of milk into his bowl. "A good inventor always puts in a little of this and a little of that," he explained.

Jessica giggled. Then she froze. She heard footsteps on the back walk. "Someone's coming!"

"Dad?" Elizabeth whispered. "Oh, no!"

"Lock the door!" Jessica yelled. "Don't let him in!"

# CHAPTER 9

# A Big Mess

Elizabeth was about to lock the back door when she saw it was only Todd. "Hi," he said as she let him in. Then he looked around the kitchen with his eyes wide. "What happened?" he asked.

"What do you mean?" Jessica asked.

Elizabeth looked around, too. Then she saw what Todd saw. There was flour and sugar on the floor, and cake batter splattered on the walls. Broken eggshells and dirty bowls were on every counter. There were even a few flour footprints across the floor!

"Oops," Elizabeth said. "We sure made a mess."

"We'll clean up after we're done," Jessica said. "Can you grease the pan, Todd?"

"Hey, no fair getting outside help," Steven said. "Todd can only watch."

Todd looked at Elizabeth and shrugged. "I'll help you clean up when you're done."

"Thanks." She gave him a big smile.

"Time to put our batter in the cake pan," Jessica said. She wiped some batter from her cheek and licked it off her finger. "Mmm. It tastes good. Is the oven ready?"

Elizabeth nodded. She looked over at her brother. "Does your cake need the same temperature as ours?" she asked.

"No," Steven said. "Anyway, I'm using the microwave oven."

Everyone turned to stare at him. "You are?" Jessica asked.

"Sure. I know all about modern technology and electronic gadgets," Steven boasted. "Remember, *I* won the science fair."

"We remember," Jessica said. "You never stop talking about it."

Steven smiled. "My cake will be done way before yours," he said.

"Don't you need a special kind of cake mix to bake in a microwave oven?" Elizabeth asked. "I've seen them at the supermarket."

"I know what I'm doing," Steven said. He poured his batter into a glass baking dish. Then he popped his cake into the microwave and punched in numbers. "Twenty minutes should be just right."

"Our cake takes forty minutes!" Jessica said. "That's twice as long!"

"That's not my problem," Steven said with a grin. He looked around the kitchen. "And this mess isn't my problem, either. You'll have to clean up my share of the kitchen. Our first bet is still on."

Before anyone could think of anything to say, Steven strolled out of the kitchen.

"Oh, brother," Elizabeth said, shaking her head.

"Come on, let's just put our cake in the oven," Jessica said.

"I'll start cleaning up," Todd said. He picked up Steven's batter-covered mixing bowl and brought it to the sink. The batter was a dark color. Todd tasted some of it. "Not too bad," he said.

Elizabeth giggled. "It's Steven's secret recipe."

Jessica was a little worried now. Steven's cake didn't have to be neater than theirs. It only had to taste better. They would just have to wait and see.

Together, the three of them swept the floor, put the dishes in the sink, and wiped the counters. When Elizabeth put the cookbook away, she peeked through the glass door of the microwave oven.

"Look," she said, pointing at Steven's cake.

Jessica and Todd crowded around to see. The batter was bubbling and popping in the pan. It looked a little bit like chocolate-colored mud. It also seemed to be shrinking instead of rising up the way a cake should.

"Yuck," Jessica said. "It looks horrible."

"You'll have to tell me tomorrow if someone asks for a second slice," Todd said.

Elizabeth looked at the oven clock. The cake had five minutes left to bake. "Do you think we should get Steven?"

"No," Jessica answered quickly. "But I can't wait for Mr. Science Expert to see his masterpiece!"

# CHAPTER 10

# Steven's Secret Recipe

"Well, that was the best birthday dinner I've ever had," Mr. Wakefield said with a big smile. "And now I have a big surprise for every—"

"Wait, Dad!" Steven said. "We have a surprise for you."

"Two surprises," Mrs. Wakefield added, smiling.

"They're birthday cakes," Jessica explained.

Elizabeth nodded. "Jessica and I made one, and Steven made one."

"I'm bringing mine in first," Steven said. He jumped out of his chair and raced out of the room.

Mr. Wakefield looked very pleased. "I don't know if I can eat another bite," he teased.

Jessica crossed her fingers. "And Daddy? We want you to say which one you like best."

"They made both cakes from scratch," their mother added. "It's another bet they made."

"Hmm . . ." Mr. Wakefield shook his head. "I don't know about this. I'll bet you anything they're both absolutely fabulous cakes."

"But you'll decide?" Jessica pleaded.

"Here it is!" Steven said, coming in again with his cake. It was very lumpy, but the chocolate frosting he had put on it made it look a little smoother.

"I'll cut you the first piece," Steven said proudly.

Jessica held her breath. If Steven's cake tasted good, he would be bossier than ever!

Steven started slicing the cake, but it seemed to be very hard. He frowned with concentration until he finally carved a tiny slice and put it on his father's plate.

"I used a recipe, but I added some secret ingredients," he explained as he began cutting more slices.

Jessica and Elizabeth watched Mr. Wakefield break off a piece of cake with his fork. It looked dry and crumbly.

"Well?" Steven asked.

Mr. Wakefield took a sip of water and then swallowed hard. "It's quite an unusual recipe, Steven," he said slowly.

Jessica looked at Elizabeth. They each tried a bite of Steven's cake. As soon as Jessica put a forkful in her mouth, she began to cough. The cake was hard and dry. It tasted terrible!

"Ugh," Jessica gasped, and gulped half a glass of milk.

"Oh, very funny," Steven said.

Elizabeth put her fork down. "Can I have some milk, please," she asked very quietly.

"Wait a second," Steven said. His face was beginning to turn red. He cut himself a piece of cake and took a bite.

"How does the cook like it?" Mrs. Wakefield asked.

Instead of answering, Steven started to cough, too.

"Yuck!" he groaned when he could talk.

65

He stared at the cake and shook his head. "That's the worst cake I ever ate!"

Everyone laughed. Soon, Steven joined in, too.

"What secret ingredients did you use?" Mrs. Wakefield asked him.

"Peanut butter and marshmallows," Steven admitted. He looked at the twins and smiled. "I guess it wasn't my best invention."

"Well, maybe it would taste just fine if you had used a regular oven," Mrs. Wakefield said. "You really do need to use a special cake mix for the microwave. Why don't you get your cake, girls?" she suggested.

"OK!" Jessica shouted. She and Elizabeth went out to the kitchen. Their cake was already on a flowered plate. It was tall and golden colored. It looked perfect.

"Happy Birthday to You!" the twins sang as they brought it out.

"Wow!" Mr. Wakefield said. "That sure is a beauty!"

Elizabeth cut the first slice and put it on their father's plate. He took one bite, chewed, and swallowed. Jessica held her breath. "Well?" she burst out.

A big smile spread across Mr. Wakefield's face. "Girls, this is absolutely, positively delicious."

"We won!" Jessica screamed. She looked at Steven. "And we don't have to do any more of your chores," she said.

Steven shrugged. "It doesn't matter." He held up his plate with a grin. "Can I have some of that cake, please?"

"First you have to say you're sorry for being so bossy," Jessica said.

"That's right," Elizabeth agreed. "You were acting really stupid."

"I'm sorry, I'm sorry, I'm sorry," Steven laughed. "Now can I please have some cake?"

Mrs. Wakefield laughed, too. "You've got him, girls. Let's pass that cake around. I have a feeling we're going to eat the whole thing right now."

"Happy birthday, Dad," Elizabeth said.

"Thank you very much," he answered, cutting himself another slice of angel food cake. "And now I have a birthday present for the whole family."

"What is it?" Jessica asked.

"To celebrate my birthday, we're going on a fishing trip," their father said. "The whole family."

"Fishing?" Elizabeth said with a smile.

"Fishing?" Steven repeated with a grin.

"*Fishing?*" Jessica repeated. She didn't sound very happy at all.

"Yes, fishing," Mr. Wakefield said. "Just like the trips Grandpa Wakefield used to take me on. Isn't everyone excited?" he asked, looking around the table.

**Who will enjoy the family fishing trip? Find out in Sweet Valley Kids # 19, JESSICA AND THE JUMBO FISH.**

# SWEET VALLEY KIDS

Jessica and Elizabeth have had lots of adventures in *Sweet Valley High* and *Sweet Valley Twins*...now read about the twins at age seven! You'll love all the fun that comes with being seven—birthday parties, playing dress-up, class projects, putting on puppet shows and plays, losing a tooth, setting up lemonade stands, caring for animals and much more! It's all part of SWEET VALLEY KIDS. Read them all!

| | | | |
|---|---|---|---|
| ☐ | SURPRISE! SURPRISE! #1 | 15758-2 | $2.75/$3.25 |
| ☐ | RUNAWAY HAMSTER #2 | 15759-0 | $2.75/$3.25 |
| ☐ | THE TWINS' MYSTERY TEACHER # 3 | 15760-4 | $2.75/$3.25 |
| ☐ | ELIZABETH'S VALENTINE # 4 | 15761-2 | $2.75/$3.25 |
| ☐ | JESSICA'S CAT TRICK # 5 | 15768-X | $2.75/$3.25 |
| ☐ | LILA'S SECRET # 6 | 15773-6 | $2.75/$3.25 |
| ☐ | JESSICA'S BIG MISTAKE # 7 | 15799-X | $2.75/$3.25 |
| ☐ | JESSICA'S ZOO ADVENTURE # 8 | 15802-3 | $2.75/$3.25 |
| ☐ | ELIZABETH'S SUPER-SELLING LEMONADE #9 | 15807-4 | $2.75/$3.25 |
| ☐ | THE TWINS AND THE WILD WEST #10 | 15811-2 | $2.75/$3.25 |
| ☐ | CRYBABY LOIS #11 | 15818-X | $2.75/$3.25 |
| ☐ | SWEET VALLEY TRICK OR TREAT #12 | 15825-2 | $2.75/$3.25 |
| ☐ | STARRING WINSTON EGBERT #13 | 15836-8 | $2.75/$3.25 |
| ☐ | JESSICA THE BABY-SITTER #14 | 15838-4 | $2.75/$3.25 |
| ☐ | FEARLESS ELIZABETH #15 | 15844-9 | $2.75/$3.25 |
| ☐ | JESSICA THE TV STAR #16 | 15850-3 | $2.75/$3.25 |
| ☐ | THE CASE OF THE SECRET SANTA<br>(SVK Super Snooper #1) | 15860-0 | $2.95/$3.50 |

# SWEET VALLEY TWINS

**Buy them at your local bookstore or use this handy page for ordering:**

Bantam Books, Dept. SVT3, 414 East Golf Road, Des Plaines, IL 60016

Please send me the items I have checked above. I am enclosing $ _____
(please add $2.50 to cover postage and handling). Send check or money
order, no cash or C.O.D.s please.

Mr/Ms _____

Address _____

City/State _____ Zip _____

SVT3-2/91

Please allow four to six weeks for delivery.
Prices and availability subject to change without notice.